ANIMALIA

Graeme Base

Within the pages of this book
You may discover, if you look
Beyond the spell of written words,
A hidden land of beasts and birds.

For many things are 'of a kind',
And those with keenest eyes will find
A thousand things, or maybe more —
It's up to you to keep the score.

A final word before we go;
There's one more thing you ought to know:
In Animalia, you see,
It's possible you might find *me*.

          — Graeme

For Robyn

Puffin Books

An Armoured Armadillo Avoiding An Angry Alligator

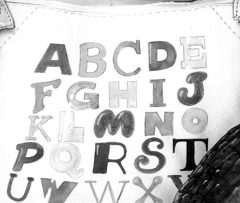

Beautiful BLUE BUTTERFLIES basking by a BABBLING BROOK

ally catching Crusty Crayfish

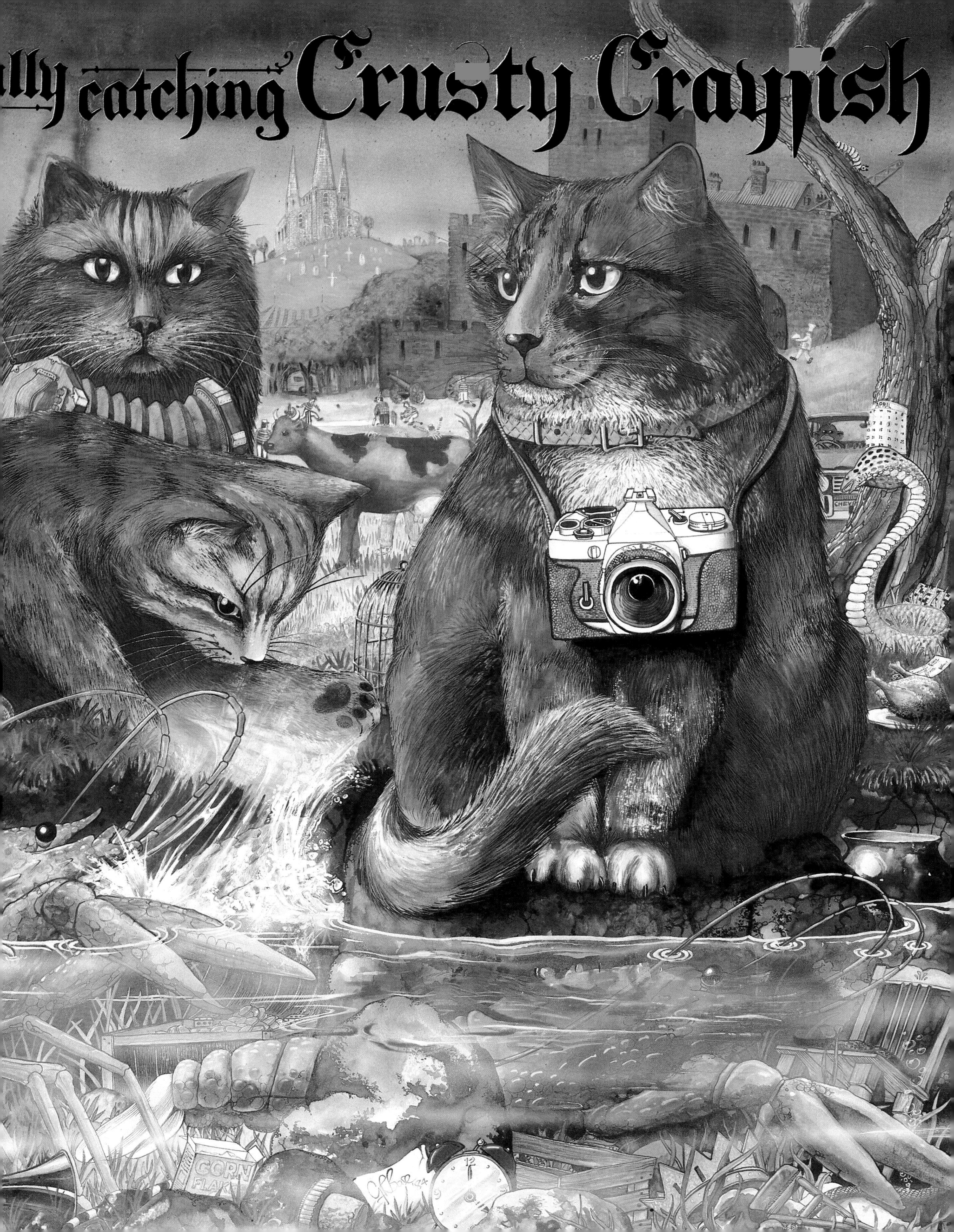

DIABOLICAL DRAGONS
DAINTILY DEVOURING
DELICIOUS DELICACIES

Quivering Quails Queuing Quietly for Quills

RICHLY ROBED RHINOCEROSES
— RIDING IN —
RICKETY RED RICKSHAWS

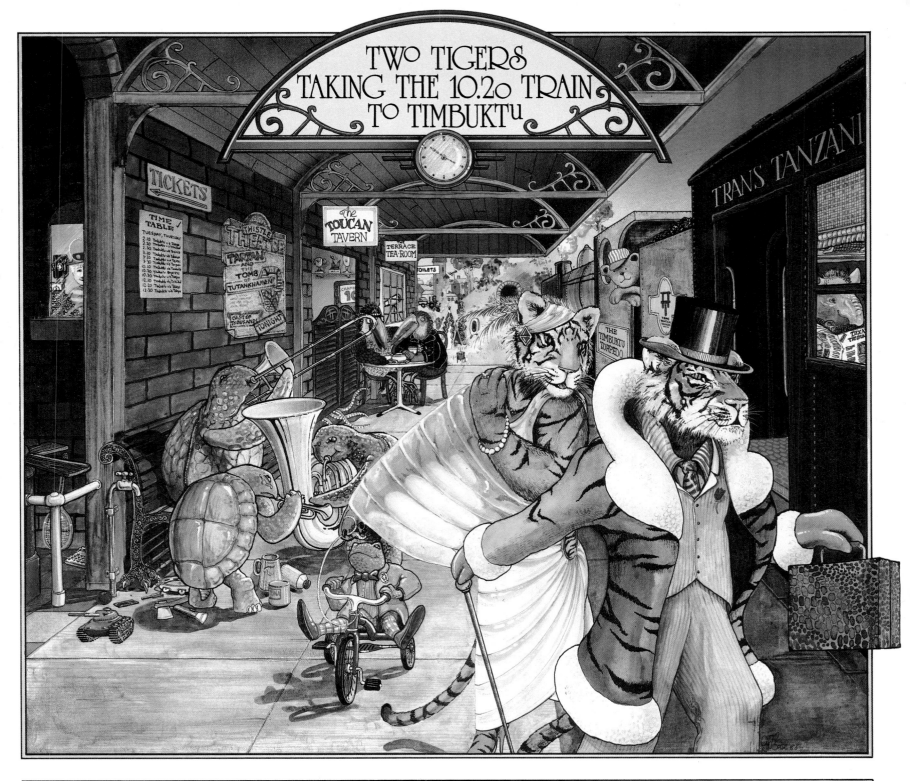

TWO TIGERS TAKING THE 10.20 TRAIN TO TIMBUKTU

UNRULY UNICORNS UPENDING URNS OF ULTRAMARINE UMBRELLAS

Wicked
Warrior
WASPS
wildly
waving
Warlike
Weapons

YOUTHFUL YAKS YODELLING IN YELLOW YACHTS

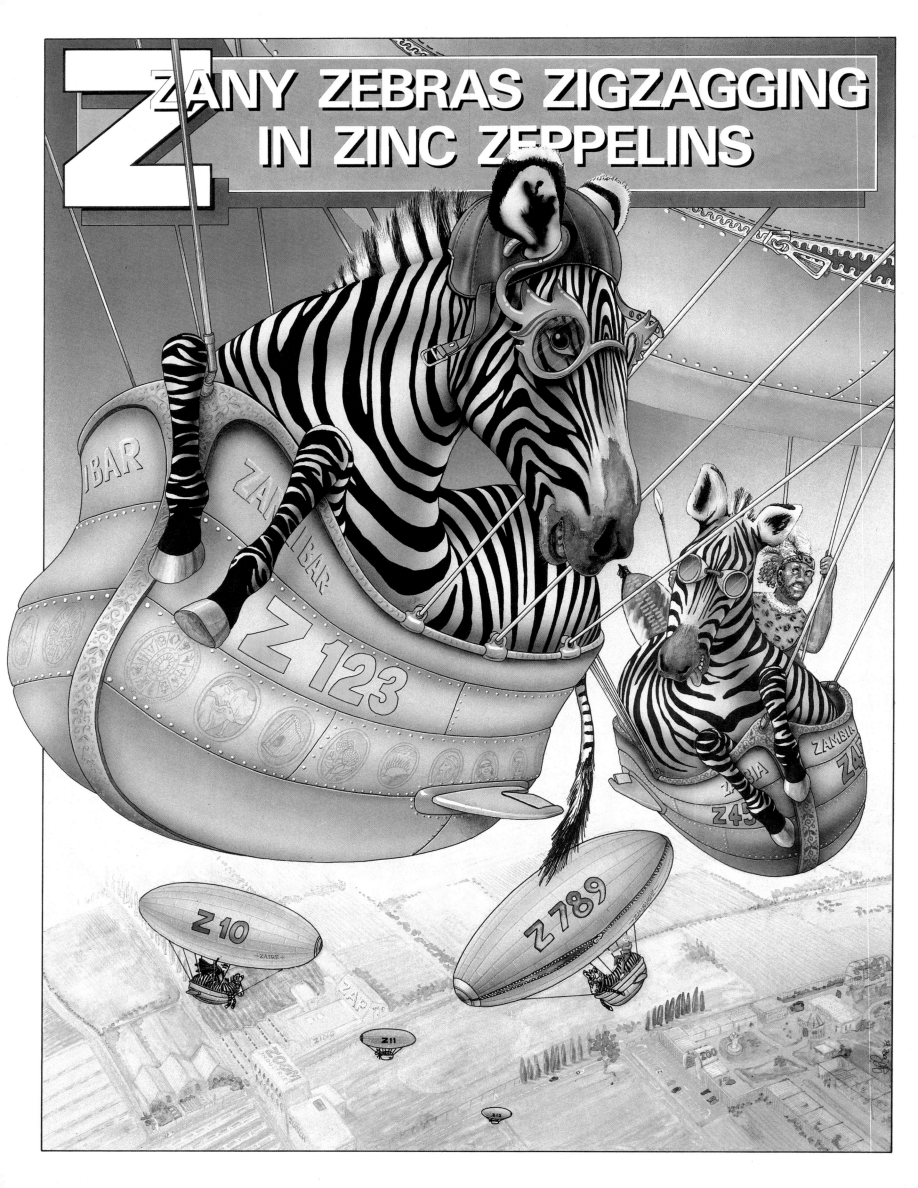

Z.
ZANY ZEBRAS ZIGZAGGING IN ZINC ZEPPELINS